My
Lil'
Chappy

Andre Pretty

Acknowledgements:

Special shout out to my wife.

Thank you for supporting me on this journey... you really
are the one in a million everyone is always talking about.

Table of Contents

Hunger

Sometimes,

The moon talks to the sun.

He whispers

Beauty

In forgotten tongues.

Caressing each flame with allegory,

And

A promise

Of subliminal wisdom.

Sunflowers **and Sundays**

Sunflowers and Sundays

Have nothing on the honey

That eagerly drips from your lips.

Your movements grace

My countenance

With an everlasting moment of

Purpose and poise.

Uniquely you and utterly perfect.

We Never Miss It

Inhale

Exhale

Breathe

&

Close your eyes.

One foot in front of the other

Fluid motion disguised as allegory.

Embracing the pain

Articulating the music with your essence.

Expressing your art by divulging in senses.

Allow your vulnerability a voice.

It's you

Yourself

&

Vibration

Swathed with

Impulsive

Ancient memory.

Painting With You

I love the color of your mind.

The shadows that envelope

The cavernous regions of intelligence

Which reside in your skull

Fascinate,

Even the most creative of wits.

You are an Oxford literary innovation,

That's entirely,

Indescribable.

Fairies Do Exist

Why do we hide from ourselves?

The audacity of people.

Audacious!

To allow their egos permission to galivant,

Rampantly!

How can you see the magic the universe

possesses,

&

Then tell yourself it's not real?

The never-ending fallacy

of humanity?

Being unable to practice

What we teach

With the integrity

That we so crave.

We say we comprehend love

While simultaneously,

Destroying the destiny

Of those who have empathy.

Those

With enough compassion

To grace us

With the gift of perception.

Imagine what it must be like,

To really see.

Maybe

Maybe.

You know the truth.

Maybe.

You finally bore witness
To genuine azimuth.

We are
The rot clinging to flesh.
We are
The horror
In the allure of existence.

We are
The demons that
Devour hopes,
Afresh.
In fact

We choose it

Want it.

Blind eyes tell no lies

Yet still scream deceit

When confronted

With the obvious

Voracity

Of being visionless.

Maybe.

We deserve it.

The plagues

&

Burdens.

The utter malevolence.

Though,

This preference for hate,

Will most certainly

Culminate our fate.

Do You Sink Too?

Some days I'm not here

Some days I disappear

                              Where are you?

Trapped like me?

                              Riddled with anxiety?

May you find comfort in the wet, electrical-controlled meat

                              That secretes

Its wants & desires

Into your very essence.

The mind,

No.

Just a prison for the neurologically challenged.

My Love Letter

Dear death,

I don't hate you.

I am grateful.

Don't you get that?

You make me want to live,

Despite you.

For you see

Without you,

I wouldn't understand the simple notion that beauty cannot
exist without tragedy.

Would it really be so bad

To surrender to the sensation of life?

Wake up. I see you.

Let me be here

&

When you finally hold me,

Please remind me,

It was all worth it.

The City

I've always preferred the city at nighttime.

I think it's the stillness of everything.

The silence that leaves me breathless.

It lingers in the air,

Lacerating my ears.

For a moment we no longer

Must pretend,

We can just

Be.

When the drunks have found their way home

&

The persistent sex starved creatures,

That lurk in the dark,

Have found companionship,

We finally see them for what they are.

Is it instinct?

We are all longing for something,

Comforting.

Something to soothe the soul that is our entirety.

Our version of the world's illusion.

I like to see the buildings stacked,

Creating tasteless arguments

That boil down to our need for survival.

Why is stagnant so reassuring?

The ricochet of my voice echoing on a faded memory hits

Different when surrounded by shadowed ally ways.

Its rich history is hidden within the smoke that stains my
Breathe

&

For one,

One

Entire moment,

        I'm uninhibited.

     I think

That's why,

        I like the city at nighttime.

Mamma Bear

You always told me you'd love me,

No matter what.

Even when I was a little dick head,

I really was.

Remember the days

I used to call you mad?

If only they knew

I meant you were my mum

& My dad.

Always there for me

Strong and true.

I don't think you ever showed

What you must have been going through.

I mean,

    I Never really knew.

You made darn sure,

    My skies were always blue.

                    I miss singing

                    The Spice Girls

                    &

                    Van Halen

                    Driving to the cabin

                    In our souped-up canary juice wagon.

Sleeping with deer and on roofs

Maybe pissing off a patrol officer,

Or two.

You're the best mom a guy could ask for.

Tough and demanding,

Even overprotective

&

A little commanding.

I think about all the kids without a mom

&

My heart breaks for them

Because

How did I get so lucky?

Why me?

Ill love you as big as the sky,

Forever your little guy.

Don't worry though

Because someday when I die

I'll know you loved me

With all your heart.

I swear,

Pinky Promise,

Double locked.

-    Forever your baby.

The Titanic Was Drunk

I promise

No one

Has a grandmother like mine

Reeking of garlic

&

Fermented wine.

Her heart is too big

For her chest.

So, she's had some work done

To counteract the neglect

Given

To her glorious self.

I love to remember

The good times with Ricco

&

Being chased around the table

By Valentino.

Hey,

Remember that time

You hit your head on the table?

Probably not

Seeing as it wasn't all that stable.

I loved to play dress up

&

Make forts under the stairs

Surrounded by pelts and layers

Of culture

&

Art

The things you've helped

Make

So dear to my heart.

Watching the titanic was probably my favorite

Even though, at the time

I kind of hated it.

I miss it now

&

Want to do it again.

You always cared about me in ways

I couldn't comprehend.

I'm just glad

You want

To spend time with me.

Because the more people that love you

The better off you'll be.

Find the Arrow

A long time ago,

I sat on a man's belly.

He pointed out,

The stars above me.

I sat in awe,

Rather disproportionately.

He told me

What they meant,

Where to find Orion's belt

&

Then he knelt.

He said if I was a good boy,

They'd never be destroyed.

I remember that man

I cared for him from the start

He gave me the gift of humility & heart.

Fresh Prince

I had always needed someone

To look up to

&

Never understood

How you could have a child then leave for good.

What did I do to you?

Is it me?

Or is it the painstaking

Reality

You'll never remedy

The seeds you sow.

I want to let go...

Of this grip.

Compressing, grinding into my soul.

I don't know you

&

I keep wishing I did

You're supposed to be in my life

But,

You're the ghost of misguided perception

Ready to plunge the knife.

Why don't you want me?

You have so many, I guess...

It doesn't matter

When you have the rest.

The ones that are normal

Not

Drowning in stress

&

Overcome

With abandonment.

I find it funny

To tell you the truth

Because

For as many role-models

                    I've had

All I've craved

Was you.

                                    I've searched

                            In people & places

                                I know

In jobs I've had

  &

Places that show

                                            Me love

                                              &

                                          Also

                                        Pain.

But you wouldn't know that

Nor

Care to partake.

                                    In the end

                        This isn't for you

                                    It's for me

                                        &

                        I hope you can see

I need to forgive you

                    In order to be free.

Dear, little Me.

Its ok.

Its ok,

To feel.

Never let them tear you apart

For It's your heart,

That makes you a man.

Dive In

Do you know any heroes?

Real ones though.

Not the ones you've been force fed to believe are the
Only righteous.

Boringly Copasetic.

No

I'm talking about real people.

People,

Whose stories are so

Brilliantly breathtaking.

The ones whose memories

Have been absorbed

Into

The universe

Awaiting the day

Broken bits of skin

&

Star dust ultimately fuse

Back together as one.

While their corpses are used

Berated,

Beaten & buried.

A cog

Beneath politics & aggravation

Of weak minds & degradation.

The glorification

That's justified by the victors

Wreaks havoc on the gentle

Mentalities that make up the stories

Worth writing down.

Expanding your reality is

Undoubtably

The precipice of understanding.

Or

In other words,

Open your

Fucking mind

&

Dive nose deep

Into the fabrication

Of this realities simulation.

Before it's too late.

Nijmegen

I've walked the footsteps
of a solider,

He died.

I heard him whisper
To me
In the early hours rise.

If I could only
Smell the blood
Weeping from the trees,

Maybe then
I'd understand
Imagined hierarchies.

The ones that kill
Innocent men
For fun.

Fun.

Wait,

Boy,
Don't forget
Your gun.

Shoot them
Kill.
Make sure you don't miss
For
Death awaits
A marauders kiss.

Don't forget Boys,
We won't be
Protecting you
After this.

You're not
A murderer.
This is war.
Nothing,
Is more important Boys.
Vainglory
We can't ignore.

I've marched the footsteps
Of my fathers' past
&
Wonder
How this could last.

The viciousness and cruelty
That comes with battle,
Leaves the innocent
Herded like cattle.

Drowning in mud
Gasping for air.
It's never been clearer
Why,
We are there.

When you slip
Into the reapers embrace,
His arms outstretched
Inviting disgrace.

Warmth,
Just a taste.

For what are we
If not alive.
We are memories intended
To thrive.

Longing for former glory,
Our story.

I've finished my walk
In the boots of this solider
Understanding more about
My composure.

I've taken the stage
&
Can see the eyes,
Of living and fallen.
Their worlds collide,

To hear me speak.

I open my throat
The words resonate
From my chest.
A backwoods route
With a familiar jest.

I've spoken my truth for all to hear

They cried
&
They cheered

But...

With the day
Crowning on its end,
I see the soldiers
Make amends.

Gliding through the mist
To eternally
Be missed,
Yet again.

Predestined.

Forever condemned
To hold their breath.
In fear of
Times sweet kiss.

Fading memories,
Cascading voices.

Calling out
In hopes the light

Will ignite

Their overdue

&

Perpetual glory.

Historical Fallacy

History's plight
Is not
Black and white

The irony of that statement is not lost
On me.

The illusion of a world doused in sepia is your minds
Reverence.

Your charlatan perception will convince you that antiquity isn't
Knocking at the door.

You've already let it in the house.

Knock! Knock!

Forget the world you think
You know
Because we know it's all a
Show.

For the weak and feeble
minded
To comprehend something

Of such grandeur,

There needs to be chaos

&

harmony.

Lap up the feverish misdirection my friends.

I sure

Wouldn't

Miss it If I were you.

Truth Bombs.

Tonight

As I lay down my head

&

Bombs fly overhead

I think about how I am expected to wake up tomorrow

& Do nothing.

        Privilege is not a foreign concept.

                This time,

           It just hits closer to home.

Knowing what I know,

Watching people sift for food in trash cans

Through my window.

I am having trouble finding the beauty I once did...

Absorbed in the malice and guilted.

I need too.

 I want too.

We must.

Stand up

For what's right.

But who can you trust when

The blood

Keeps pooling

Under weighted opinions of men

Who've never set foot in sight,

Of reality.

I am nowhere near

Understanding the plight

Of people born

Emersed in this endless fight.

It pains me to grasp

The lack of compassion

The world has to offer

To those in need

Of saving.

Be Gone Demon.

When the damage
Is all said and done,

&
It's time to say goodbye

To the sun,

Will you realize
The lies
You've been told
In order,
To mold

This demonized
Version
Of the world?

Or will you finally see,
We are all worthy

Of a life
With no hold?

Asking a Fish

To Climb a Tree.

Evolution.

They say humans have proven our evolution Throughout
time
With our wisdom & development of tools.

You know what I say?

That's bullshit.

The first time we held each other.
When we really
Truly
Felt pain.

Understanding,
The pain of agony and anguish.

The pain of loss and revenge.

That
Is the testament.

The testament to our ability
To comprehend
Our universe around us.

This apparent "higher" intellect we've lain claim to,
It's a lie.

We are the ones

Who have come up with the test.

The first fixed femur.
Do you know what that means?

It means

We didn't leave someone behind.

We realized the usefulness beyond that of ourselves.

We fucking cared,

& That,

That

Is what makes us so darn special.

What makes us innately,

Human.

Merciless Positivity

Sometimes life
is hard but that does not
mean it's impossible.

There are going to be times when you will break.

I promise you
though,

You won't be
broken.

You have the inner strength of heroes.

Even if,

It's buried under apprehension

&

Humanity.

Allow the waning doubt
to ignite the fire
thundering from your
chest.

Do it.

All that's needed,

Is a spark.

One

Ember

To spiral

& Be

The BECON!

The light,

In   our
moments   of
discontent.

Thrive   in   the   unremitting
underestimation.

&

Never surrender.

You are
stronger   than
you think.

Ramblings of a Crusty Philosopher

Interconnection

Direction

Let's expand on the universe's vibration

Intergalactic philosophic annihilation

Or

Are you addicted to the viral perception, the misdirection,

Speculating the pain and prophetic demise of

Our own creation

Deviation

A novel experience is soon a reflex

Subconscious, unconscious, it sounds obvious

To say my consciousness

But

How can you prove

I'm here?

How many miles

Will I have to walk

Witness the shoes, it'll take

To be fully awake

Who takes the reigns when the chemicals react

In fact, is it still the nervous system,

A bodily reaction

Or just another thing

To add

To this so-called interaction

With existence, coincidence

They say there is no experience except consciousness itself

I challenge you to find the interconnected self,

Well-being

Meaning,

The people who forsake the warm gift of life

Are In favor of the flavorless

Forever dancing in the realm

Of Nihilists.

Don't let your independent film be cut short

No director can take your voice.

This is your opportunity

Your choice.

I don't believe in God.

I don't believe in God.

I don't think I ever could.

How can you justify

The lack there of good.

We revel in pain,

Evil and savagery.

We lie and lust for
blood and glory.

Stuck in continual,

Unbridled forgery.

How can there be

An entity such as he

Who wishes depravations upon thee?

I was once told,

I'd be embraced & adored,

In a kingdom of gold.

Yet as the years unfold

I continue to become

Consciously aware

Of the lies

&

Utter dismay.

The crumbling mountains,

&

Scenes of shattered fountains

Pouring a deep crimson display.

I don't believe in God.

I don't think I ever did,

Even when I mimed my prayers

As a little kid.

I've had time to comprehend

The corruption,

The Degradation

Of good

&

Honest men.

It's not a serpent

Or a big poof in the sky

In which we find

Internal lies.

Only if you look

Close enough

To see,

Then

Ask questions.

Will you then

Be able

To accept the truth.

That is

Humans,

Innately,

Search for clues.

The forces that drive us,

The choices

Beneath our actions.

We often place blame

Instead of

Reflection

&

Reaction.

Why is there

This

Horrid misconception?

To understand

That YOU are

In charge of

YOUR life

&

That alone

Holds you

Accountable

In strife.

It's liberating,

Intimidating

Simultaneously explosive.

Yet...

We are so insignificant

In the grandeur,

That is existence.

It's our humanity

That keeps us

Persistent,

In our ever growing

Search for erudition.

It can't be

One perception

Guiding the misdirection,

That created what we see.

There's no way

In actuality.

All that's known

For certain?

The universe has

Truly created,

Undiluted burden.

About The Author

Andre Pretty is the most underestimated S. O. B alive. He's a ridiculously well-travelled army brat whose passion for writing finally caught up with him, not to mention, his international studies, athletics and various University/College courses have given a unique perspective. The experiences gained from life are delicious, enticing, and if you're still here get ready to experience fluency. With hero's ranging from Robin Williams to Diogenes his personality screams flavor and, as they say, never judge a book by its cover. This guy right here is no exception. If ever you can't find him just look to the Rockies or at his favorite pub in the lovely YYC. Lastly, I'll leave you with this little tidbit to suck on, if he brings home any more stray animals his wife will probably file for divorce. My Lil' Chappy is Andres first poetry book and won't be the last. He's currently working on two other works of fiction so make way for the newest writer on the block and, you had best get acquainted with last name Pretty.

Made in the USA
Coppell, TX
12 March 2022

74878026R00038